ARTHUR'S SCIENCE FAIR TROUBLE

亚瑟的"创意模型"

（美）马克·布朗　绘著

范晓星　译

CHISO 新疆青少年出版社

On the first day of school,
Mr. Ratburn told his class
about the science fair.
"I want each of you
to do a science project.
On Parents' Night
the best project will get
a blue ribbon."

"I'm going to make a rocket
for my project," said Buster.
"Oh, nuts!" said Arthur.
"That's what I was going to do."
"I'm sorry," said Buster.
"That's okay," said Arthur.
"I can think of something else."

4

Weeks passed.

Everyone had a project—

everyone but Arthur.

"I'm growing crystals.

They look just like diamonds,"

said Muffy.

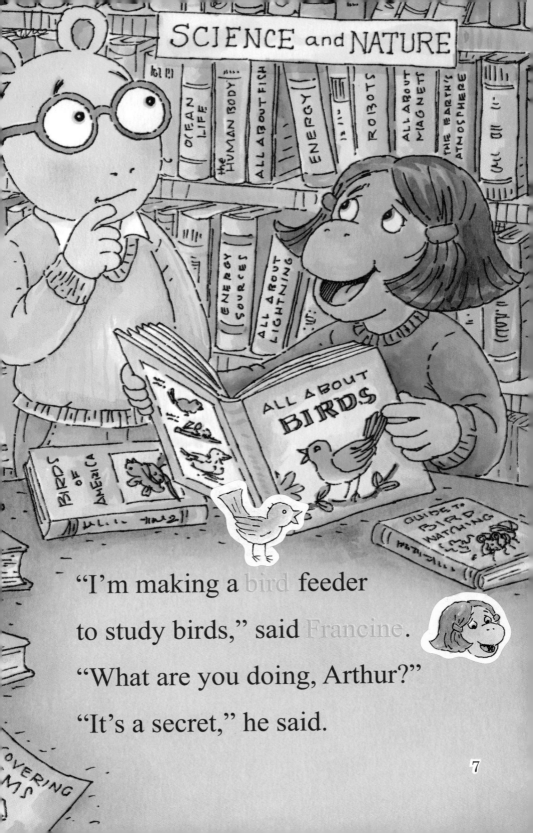

"I'm making a bird feeder
to study birds," said Francine.
"What are you doing, Arthur?"
"It's a secret," he said.

That night D.W. wanted
Arthur to play Go Fish.
"I can't," he said. " I have to think
of a science project for Monday!"
"The attic is full
of Dad's old projects,"
said D.W. "If you're smart,
you'll ask him for help."
"No help allowed," said Arthur.

After D.W. went to bed,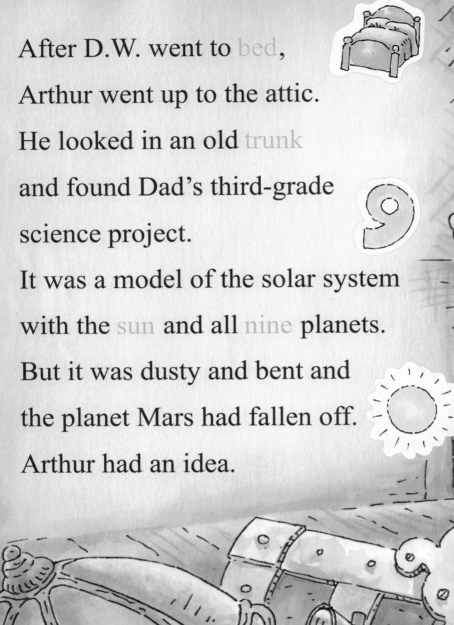
Arthur went up to the attic.
He looked in an old trunk
and found Dad's third-grade
science project.
It was a model of the solar system
with the sun and all nine planets.
But it was dusty and bent and
the planet Mars had fallen off.
Arthur had an idea.

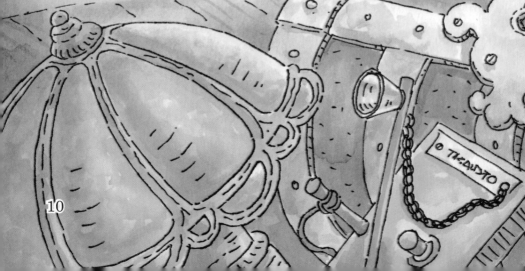

Over the weekend
Arthur cleaned the model.
He glued Mars back in place.
He painted the sun orange.
He painted each of the planets
a different color.

Monday morning everyone
took their projects
to the lunchroom.
"Yours is the best,"
said Buster.

"Oh, no!" said Arthur.

"Oh, yes!" said Francine.

"I bet it gets the blue ribbon,"

said the Brain.

Suddenly Arthur felt sick.

All afternoon Arthur wanted
to tell Mr. Ratburn the truth.
After school Arthur said,
"I need to talk to you…."
"Got to run. I'm late
for my dentist,"
said his teacher. "We can talk
tonight at Parents' Night."

Arthur ate his dinner slowly.

Very slowly.

"Hurry up," said his dad.

"We don't want to be late

for Parents' Night."

But they were late.

"And the blue ribbon

goes to Arthur Read,"

said Mr. Ratburn.

Now Arthur felt really sick.

"Amazing," said Dad.

"It looks like the project

I did in third grade."

"It is the project you did,"

said Arthur. "I just fixed it

and painted it.

I'm really sorry."

Dad just shook his head.

"I think," said Mr. Ratburn.

"the blue ribbon should now go

to Arthur's father.

As for Arthur,

he has some explaining to do…

and a science project of his own."

D.W. said, "Oh, boy, Arthur,

you're in trouble."

And Dad said, "Arthur has to do
even more explaining
when we get home."
"Now you're in double trouble,"
said D.W.

译文

2. 开学第一天，舒老师向全班同学布置了科学模型展的任务：

"同学们，我要你们每个人都动手做一个科学模型。等到'家长之夜'，做得最好的同学将得到一枚蓝带勋章。"

4. "我打算做一支火箭。"巴斯特说。

"讨厌，"亚瑟说，"我也想做火箭！"

"对不起啊。"巴斯特赶紧道歉。

"没关系，我再想想别的吧。"亚瑟回应。

6. 转眼一星期过去了，除了亚瑟，其他同学都想好了科学模型的主题。

"我想做一个水晶生长实验，瞧，它们看上去多像钻石呀！"玛菲说。

7. "我想做一个喂鸟器，然后用它来了解鸟类。"芳馨说，"你打算做什么呢，亚瑟？"

"暂时保密。"亚瑟回答。

8. 晚上，朵拉要亚瑟陪她一起玩儿纸牌。

"不行，我还要想星期一的科学模型主题呢！"亚瑟说。

"阁楼上到处都是爸爸小时候做过的科学模型，"朵拉说，"你不是特聪明吗，干吗不去找爸爸帮忙呀？"

"不可以找人帮忙的。"亚瑟回答。

10. 等朵拉上床睡觉去了，亚瑟悄悄爬上阁楼。在一个旧箱子里，他发现了爸爸三年级时做的一个科学模型。

那是一个有关太阳和九大行星的太阳系模型，模型上落满了灰尘，有的地方还被压瘪了，火星也脱落了。

亚瑟脑子里闪过一个主意。

13. 整个周末，亚瑟都在忙着拾掇模型。

他把火星粘了回去，把太阳涂成橘红色，又把每颗行星都涂上了不同的颜色。

14. 星期一早上，同学们都把自己的科学模型送到餐厅去布置展览。
"你的模型最棒了！"巴斯特说。
15. "你开玩笑的吧？"亚瑟回应。
"没错，真的很棒！"芳馨说。
"我敢说，它一定能为你赢得蓝带勋章。"小灵通也说。
亚瑟忽然觉得心里有些七上八下的。

16. 整个下午，亚瑟都想告诉舒老师实话。

总算放学了，亚瑟对舒老师说："我想和您谈谈……"

"我得走了，我要去看牙医，快迟到了。"舒老师回应，"今晚'家长之夜'咱们再聊吧。"

18. 亚瑟晚餐吃得慢吞吞的，要多慢有多慢。

"快一点，"爸爸说，"今晚'家长之夜'，我们可不能迟到呀。"

19. 不过，他们还是迟到了。

"蓝带勋章得主是亚瑟·李德同学！"舒老师宣布。

亚瑟一颗心提到了嗓子眼儿。

20. "好奇怪呀！"爸爸说，"这个模型就和我三年级时做的那个一模一样。"

"这就是您做的那个，"亚瑟小声回应，"我只不过把它修好了，又涂了一遍颜色。我现在可后悔了。"

爸爸一个劲地摇头。

30

22. "我看，"舒老师说，"这枚蓝带勋章应该发给亚瑟的爸爸。至于亚瑟嘛，你必须好好向我们大家解释这件事……而且还要补做一个真正属于你自己的科学模型。"

朵拉嘀咕："哎哟，天哪，哥哥，你可有大麻烦啦。"

24. 爸爸说："回家以后，亚瑟还得好好向全家人解释这件事。"

"哥哥，麻烦成双喽！"朵拉惊呼。